I0692185

Whose A&& Is That?

This book is a work of fiction. Any references to historical events, real people, or real locales are used fictitiously. Other names, characters, places, and incidents are the product of the author's imagination, and any resemblance to actual events or locales or persons, living or dead, is entirely coincidental.

Illustrated by Traycee Bosle

Book design by Sherry Linger Kaier

The Artists' Orchard, LLC
P.O. Box 113317
Pittsburgh, PA 15241

www.theartistsorchard.com

ISBN: 978-0-9857014-4-4

Library of Congress Control Number: 2013934318

Produced and Printed in the United States of America

For my grandmother, Samena Muraco Sarne, who

called me contrary
observed the three second rule
grew rhubarb
fell asleep at night listening to talk radio
buried two children
whizzed through crossword puzzles
watched studio wrestling
disciplined with a wooden spoon
crocheted
had an arranged marriage
wore her braided white hair tucked in a chignon

Whose Ass Is That?

Every woman or so I'm told

whether in her twenties or many years old

has a love-hate relationship with her hiney,

be it extra-venti or teeny tiny.

Lest you think I might be loose

because I speak of my caboose,

I figure – it's there,

so why despair?

I will honor it a-la Dr. Seuss.

Ah yes, at some point I began to steer clear
of the dreaded full-length mirror.

This went on for years and years.

Some things are, uh, larger than they appear.

I avoided the image I knew I would see

of what was growing right behind me.

Yet there once was a time

when my bum was the bomb,

woe is me, those days have long since gone.

Back in the day men used to stare

at my perfectly perky derriere.

I didn't think twice about seeing it bare

or adorned with sparkly underwear.

Strolling with friends, the cars would honk

at our short-short, jean-clad badonk-a-donks.

I used to think,

"What's all the fuss?"

After all, there is a bottom on each of us.

Then one day just a few years back

a glimpse of my tush stopped me in my tracks.

I wondered aloud, "Whose ass is that?!

And when did it get so wide and flat?"

From that day on

I've diligently tried

the best I could

to thoroughly hide

my ample, bee-stung, swollen back side.

You've heard of the phrase CYA, have you not?

Well it started with me and the can that I've got.

Amuse me a bit as I share with you how

I attempt to cover my arse even now.

Being covert I try to divert

attention away from my tail

with billowy wraps that flutter and flap

but of course,

to no avail.

In wintertime though, I get a reprieve

as bulky clothing helps to deceive.

I layer up woolies

to cover my coolie.

Does that fool you, or am I naïve?

I often squoosh my bubble tush

into my favorite jeans.

When I do,

between me and you,

yes, I strain the seams.

Will they ever fit again?

Of course...

In my dreams!

Tush

Booty

Hiney

Rump

Bum

Keister

Caboose

Bottom

I know.

It's obvious I seem obsessed

with the bountiful gluteus maximus

of which I have been generously blessed.

Being open minded, I certainly declare that some may wish for more back there.

If someone were to ask me, I'd gladly share.

Believe me, I've got plenty to spare.

So many foods I find hard to resist

But they find their way onto my grocery list

then into my mouth...

then onto my hips...

then take up shop on...

you've guessed it...

and I'm pissed.

I've tried to whittle my oversize dupa

by shaking my hips with my hula-hoopa

I twist and I turn as

the calories burn

in hopes of it lifting up all the droopa.

I bought all the gizmos from late night TV
that promise to shape and redefine me.
They sit in a corner piled into a heap.
Money wasted when I just couldn't sleep.

Where are all those books

I've read over time

ensuring my rear view

would be sublime?

They sold at my yard sale last year

for a dime.

Pardon me as I stand by the hedge

and discreetly tug to get rid of my wedge.

It's a problem for others too, I allege.

The solution could be loin cloths.

They have no elastic edge.

While I'm talking undies,

knickers,

gutchies,

drawers,

skivvies,

boy shorts,

panties,

or whatever you call yours,

I'll admit that what irks me most, no doubt:

lacy little thong straps

accidentally peeking out.

Yet for all that I've gone and babbled about,

my butt is a part I can't do without.

It cushions my falls and fills out my pants

and I need it to shake when I get up and dance.

It follows me wherever I go,

my bum,

my tookus,

my prodigious popo.

Like the wrinkles upon my face,

and sagging in another place,

I've come to terms and will with grace,

genuinely embrace that who I am

is not defined

by the size of

my behind.

The ~~End~~ Backside

Author
Marylu Zuk

A western Pennsylvania native, author Marylu Zuk settled in sunny Arizona for a decade before boomeranging back to Pittsburgh where she lives with her husband and son. She spent the early part of her career in the sometimes friendly skies perfecting the art of smiling through anything - at least until she was out of the passengers' sight. (Really sir? You actually need me to buckle your seat belt for you?) Her life's path has taken her from babysitter, to playground supervisor, flight attendant, road warrior, workshop presenter, sales manager and enrollment VP. The titles may have changed, but the job responsibilities did not – maintain order and keep people happy. While getting ready for a promotions event a few years back, Marylu used the two-mirror trick to see how she looked in her jeans. 'Oh my God! Whose ass is that?!' she exclaimed … and the idea for her first book was born. **Whose A&& is That?** invites every woman to relax her abs, exhale, and laugh at what we rarely see – our own backsides!

Illustrator
Traycee Bosle

Traycee is an artist and illustrator with a talent for weaving a visual story. Her illustrations often feature soft lines, bright colors, and a whisper of whimsy. A graduate of the Art Institute of Pittsburgh, she juggles a professional career in marketing with her passions for fine art and literature. She lives with her husband and two young children in Pittsburgh, Pennsylvania.

©Rich Waters Photography

Acknowledgement

The list of those I owe my appreciation is long, and I fear that if I mention each by name, I would forget someone. I have been fortunate to cross paths with many special people in this life – my family, friends, colleagues, mentors, teachers, guides, and simpatico compadres. Know that if you are reading this, I am grateful for you.

Be happy. Be kind. Pay it forward.

Marylu